Edwin Whitefield

The Homes of our Forefathers

Being a selection of the oldest and most interesting buildings, historical

houses, and noted places in Rhode Island and Connecticut

Edwin Whitefield

The Homes of our Forefathers

Being a selection of the oldest and most interesting buildings, historical houses, and noted places in Rhode Island and Connecticut

ISBN/EAN: 9783337381295

Printed in Europe, USA, Canada, Australia, Japan

Cover: Foto ©Andreas Hilbeck / pixelio.de

More available books at **www.hansebooks.com**

THE HOMES

of our

FOREFATHERS.

BEING A SELECTION OF THE

Oldest and Most Interesting Buildings, Historical Houses,
and Noted Places in Rhode Island and Connecticut.

FROM ORIGINAL DRAWINGS MADE ON THE SPOT

EDWIN WHITEFIELD.

WHITEFIELD AND CROCKER,
25 BROMFIELD STREET.
1882.

TO THE READER.

THE object of this book is to preserve and hand down to all future generations representations of the Homes of their Forefathers. From a variety of causes they are rapidly disappearing; and before long the places that now know them will know them no more. It has been a labor of love to the undersigned to collect these mementoes of the past, and his efforts have been ably seconded by many gentlemen to whom his thanks are hereby returned. He has labored under many disadvantages which cannot be here enumerated: but he has tried to do his work faithfully, and no liberties have been taken with the old buildings represented, or with their surroundings, merely for pictorial effect. It is true that a few houses have been slightly altered from what they *are* to what they *were* originally; and sometimes an indifferent object, such as an old barn, or it may be a tree, has been left out or pushed aside to show the building to better advantage. Thus, if not photographically correct, they are sufficiently so for all practical purposes.

With these preliminary remarks he respectfully offers his book to all who are interested in the early history of those who laid the foundations of New England, trusting it will meet with their approval.

E. WHITEFIELD.

READING, MASS., March, 1882.

DATES OF IMPORTANT EVENTS

IN THE

EARLY HISTORY OF NEW ENGLAND.

The Bull House, Newport, R. I.

This is probably the oldest house now standing in Rhode Island, having been built in 1639. The above view represents it as it was before the recent changes had been made in it; although it is probable the roof is more modern than the rest of the house. The greater portion is built of stone, and it has been partially plastered over. It stands on Spring Street.

The Atkinson House, Newport, R. I.

This is a very old and interesting house with an immense stone chimney, probably built by one of the Easton family about 1645, but this fact cannot be established. By some it has been said to have been built by a Robinson, but it has been traced back to 1745, and it was an old house then. It stands in the rear of Thames St., near Mary St. The stones of which the chimney is built are similar to those used in the Old Mill.

The Bishop Berkley House, Newport, R.I.

This well-known mansion, which was occupied by the celebrated Bishop Berkley during his residence in this part of America, is about 3 miles out of Newport, and has been very little changed from its original condition.

Channing's Birth-place, Newport, R.I.

This was the birth-place of the Rev. Dr. Channing, whose name and fame are indelibly impressed on the ecclesiastical annals of New England. This house stands at the corner of Mary and School Streets; and, as represented here, shows it in its original condition before the queer addition to the roof was put on.

The Bosworth House, Bristol, R.I.

This house was built by Deacon Bosworth, 1680. It afterwards became the property of Judge Bourne, and is now owned by Mrs. Jas. Perry. This is not only a very old house, but highly interesting in many respects.

Reynold's House, Bristol, R.I.

This was built by Jas. Reynolds about 1700, and has never passed out of the possession of his descendants. The interior decorations and fittings-up of this house are very peculiar. It is also noted for having been the headquarters of La Fayette when in this neighborhood.

Blackstone's Grave, Lonsdale, R.I.

The two stones in the foreground of the picture mark the grave of Blackstone, the first settler of what is now the City of Boston. This is in the outskirts of the Village of Lonsdale, in an open field, beside a little brook. It is strange that a monument has not long since been erected to his memory.

The Williams House, Providence, R.I.

This house, built by Jos. Williams, son of Roger Williams, is situated near the Roger Williams Park. It is claimed to have been erected in 1652; and the glass in some of the upper windows is said to have been brought from England by Roger W. on his second visit there in 1662.

Tillinghast Mansion, Providence, R. I.

Parson Tillinghast, who came to Rhode Island 1645, built the first Baptist Church in Providence. Philip, his second son, built this house about 1710. It must have been at that time one of the finest houses in Providence. It is still owned by his descendants, and is 299 South Main street.

Whipple or Abbott House, Providence, R. I.

This is claimed to be the oldest building now standing in Providence, and is believed to have been built by Roger Mowry about 1659, and he sold it to Samuel Whipple 1671. It afterwards passed into the possession of the Abbott family, and is now (1881) owned by John Comb. It stands on Abbott street.

The Phillips Mansion, Wickford, R. I.

This stands near the Belleville Station, and was built about 1698 by a wealthy man named Phillips, who came here from Newport. The large stone chimney is a very remarkable one. The present windows are much larger than the original ones.

Updike House, Wickford, R. I.

This is a famous old house. It was originally a block-house, built by Capt. Smith about 1660, and after his death, came into the possession of his son-in-law, —— Updike. It has since been enlarged and considerably altered.

The Eddy House, Warren, R. I.

This is probably the oldest brick house now standing in Warren. It is situated on Washington St. It has until recently belonged to the Eddy family, and is probably about 130 years old. The chimney is quite peculiar, being built on the outside of the house.

The Hazard House, St. Kingston, R. I.

This was built by Geo. Hazard, great-grandfather of the present owner. Thos. J. Hazard, about 1730. It is very pleasantly situated on what is called Boston Neck, and is a large and handsome mansion.

The Paine House, Conanicut, R.I.

This is a picturesque old building on Conanicut Park Farm, said to have been built by Capt. Thos. Paine, who married one of Gov. Carr's daughters. It must be about 180 years old. Many silly stories have been told about this place in connection with Capt. Kidd.

The Carr House, Conanicut, R.I.

This is a singular old place, consisting of two buildings, one frame, and the other stone; the latter having an immense stone chimney, and doubtless the older portion. It was probably built by Gov. Carr for his son, nearly 200 years ago.

.

Cæsar House, Providence, R. I.

This was probably built by Widow Penelope Green, between 1750 and 1744, and soon after bought by Wm. Cæsar, a colored man, and still owned by his descendents. It stands on corner of Main and Howes Street.

Coddington House, Newport, R. I.

This is believed to be a pretty correct representation of one of the first houses built on the island, about 1650, or perhaps a little later. It has been pulled down some years since.

Fenner House, Johnston, R. I.

This is a very dilapidated old mansion, built by Thos. Fenner about 1668, and used as a garrison house. It is uninhabited and fast going to ruin.

The Governor Greene House, E. Greenwich, R. I.

One portion of this was built in 1685 by Saml. Gorton, Jr., and the other part by Wm. Greene, Jr., in 1750.

The Old Ballou Church, Cumberland, R. I.

This was built by Maturin M. Ballou, an ancestor of President Garfield's mother, about the year 1700.

King House, Newport, R. I.

The eastern portion of this was built in 1711 by Capt. Wm. Langley; the next owner was Capt. Handy, and from his heirs, Dr. David King bought it. It stands on Pelham Street.

The Whitfield House, Guilford, Conn.

This was built in 1639, by the Rev. Henry Whitfield, and is the oldest house now standing in Conn. The walls and chimney are stone, and there is no other old house in N. England to be compared with it for durability. It was undoubtedly built for the double purpose of a dwelling and a fort. It stands on high ground not far from the R.R. Station and commands an extensive view. It has had several owners, and now belongs to Mrs. Cone, of Old Stockbridge, Mass.

The Griswold House, Guilford.

This was built by William Seward between 1655 and 1660. The chimney is stone. It was bought by the Lees of the Seward family, and afterwards came into the possession of the Griswolds, being now owned by Mrs. Griswold.

The Saltonstall House, Branford, Conn.

This was built by Rev. Gurdon Saltonstall, in 1708, soon after his appointment as Governor. It passed out of the hands of his descendants in 1775, and has gone through many changes since that time.

The Roger Sherman House, New Haven.

This was built by Roger Sherman, one of the signers of the Declaration of Independence. It remains still in possession of his descendants, and has not been materially changed from its original condition. It stands on Chapel street, nearly opposite Yale College.

The Huntington House, Norwich Town.
This is said to have been built by Christopher Huntington nearly 200 years ago. Five generations of the Huntingtons were born in this house, but it has passed out of their possession.

The Dr. Turner Place, Norwich Town.
This was the residence of Dr. Philip Turner, Surgeon-General of the Eastern Department in the War of the Revolution. It was a very old building when he purchased it, 1765, and is probably at least 150 years old. It is now the property of two of his descendents, John Turner Wait and Jonathan Turner Bull.

The Denison House, Stonington.

Three brothers of this family came over from England, of whom one named George settled in Conn., and his son John probably built this house about 200 years ago. It is fast going to ruin.

This is in the town of Stonington, near Mystic Bridge.

The Mortimer Mansion, Middletown, Conn.

This, in its best days, was a very fine place on high ground, overlooking the Connecticut River, with an avenue of splendid trees, but is now going fast to ruin. It was built by Philip Mortimer, about 1750.

The Boardman House, Rocky Hill, Conn.

This is a very peculiar old house, and was probably built at least 150 years ago by one of the Boardmans, who were early settlers in the town of Wethersfield, of which Rocky Hill was formerly a part.

The Rollins House, Rocky Hill.

This is claimed to be the first brick house built in Conn. of bricks made in the state. It was erected by Jno. Robbins in 1767, who at the time was one of the richest men in the state. Two of his sons fought in the battle of Bunker Hill. He was descended from Jno. Robbins, who came from England to Wethersfield in 1638.

The Clark or Porter House Farmington.

This house was probably built by John Clark before 1700 and it remained in the Clark family until 1794, when it was sold to Romanta Norton, who in 1798 sold it to Shubael Porter. It was pulled down 1830. It stood on the east side of High St.

The Whitman House, Farmington.

This is the oldest house now standing in Farmington. It was bought by the present Mr. Whitman's great great grandfather in 1732, and was several years old then, so that it is probably at least 170 years old. This is the only house now left in Conn. having Pendants attached to the front projection.

Scovill or Johnson House, Waterbury.

This was built as early as 1720, if not before, by John Scovill, one of the first settlers, for his son William. In 1773 it passed into the possession of Dr. Abner Johnson, and is now owned by some of his great-grandchildren. Dr. Johnson was the first apothecary in this part of the country, and he and his wife made many of their drugs.

Arnold House, New Haven.

This was built by Benedict Arnold, the Traitor, in 1771, and he left it in 1776. In after years it was owned by Noah Webster, who lived here from 1802 to 1812, when he sold it to Fred. Hunt for $5,450, and it is still in possession of his heirs. It stands on Water Street, and has seen its best days. Arnold bought the land of Sheriff Mansfield, whose daughter he married

Winthrop Mansion and Mill, New London.

The mill was erected in 1650 by John Winthrop, but the house was built by a descendant of his, John Still Winthrop, in 1750, and is a spacious mansion, standing on elevated ground and surrounded by fine trees.

Hempstead House, New London.

This is one of the few houses which escaped the burning of New London by Arnold in 1780. It was built about 1643 by Joshua Hempstead, and his descendants of the eighth generation still live in it. It is a very interesting old building, and is still in good repair.

The Patterson House, Berlin.

This was built by Isaac Hart about 150 years ago, and is now owned by Miss Abby Patterson. It is about a mile from the R.R. Station.

The Beckly House, Berlin.

This was formerly a tavern, and Washington is said to have stopped here. It is believed to be about 175 years old.

Deserted Mansion, Vernon.

This is a very dilapidated old place, and must soon fall unless it is pulled down. It was probably built by — Hunt about 1730

Old Tavern & Store, Bolton Conn.

This was a busy place during the Revolutionary War, a vast amount of teaming being done along this highway. It is now a farm house merely, belonging to Calvin Carver, and is about 130 years old It stands 1½ mile from Bolton Station.

The Gov. Walcott House, Litchfield.

This was the residence of the first Gov. Walcott, who built it about 1753. It stands near the center of the village, and is a fine old house in a good state of preservation.

The Gould House, Litchfield.

This was built by Hon. Elisha Sheldon, 1760. He moved from Lyme to Litchfield in 1753, and was a prominent man in both town and State. His son Elisha was a Colonel in the Continental army, and Washington staid at this house when in Litchfield. In 1780 Gen. Uriah Tracy bought this house and put on its present high roof; and afterwards his son-in-law, Judge Joseph Gould, became the owner and established the celebrated Litchfield Law-School. A few years since it again changed hands, and Prof. James M. Hoppin of Yale College purchased and still owns it. It commands a charming view of the lake and western hills.

The Kingsbury House, Waterbury.
This house stands on North Main street, and belongs to W. C. D.
Kingsbury, and must be upwards of 100 years old; but, like its possessor,
it has been well preserved.

The Adams, or Chapman House, Waterbury.
This house, built by Luke Adams, is said to have been the first frame
house built in Waterbury. It is about a mile from the city, and on the
turnpike leading to Watertown. It was originally of one story, but was
raised about 90 years since by John Adams to its present dimensions, on
the occasion of his marriage to a second wife. It now belongs to the Chip-
man family.

The Hurlbut House, Winchester.
This is a stone-house situated in the woods not far from the Reservoir,
and about one and a half miles out of Winsted.   The date is uncertain,
but it is said to be upward of one hundred years old.

John Brown's Birthplace, Torrington.
John Brown, one of the noblest victims to Southern slavery, was born
here 1800.   His father, Owen Brown, five years afterwards moved to
Ohio.   This was an old house when John Brown's father bought it, and
is probably about 120 or 130 years old.   The Brown family was worthily
descended from one of that name who came to Plymouth, 1621.

Jackson House, Derby, Conn.

This is one of the oldest buildings now to be found in Derby, and was built by Jackson, one of the original settlers, or by his immediate descendants, about the year 1730 or 1740. The views from this house are very fine.

Old Academy, Derby, Conn.

This was for many years a famous Academy, and pupils came here from the West Indies and other foreign countries. But its glory has departed, and it is now used as a tenement house. The situation is very fine, commanding as it does lovely views of the Housatonic and Naugatuck valleys. It was built about 1770.

Rowley or Lacey House, Bridgeport, Conn.

This represents the house as it was originally. It was built by Deacon Henry Rowley considerably upwards of one hundred years ago. It afterwards passed into the possession of the Lacey family, and is now owned by Henry Blakeman.

Nichols House, Bridgeport, Conn.

This is believed to have been built by Philip Nichols before the Revolution, when he and his father were the only traders in this part of the country. This was then a part of Stratford, and vessels came up to a wharf and store-houses (now gone) at the water seen in the view. The house is now owned by Noah Plum.

The Clark House, Stratford.

This house stands on Main St., and is believed to have been built by — Clark about 200 years ago. It is now (1881) owned by Mrs. Dayton. Col. Russ was quartered here during a portion of the Revolutionary War.

The Judson House, Stratford.

This is claimed to have been built by Will Judson, who settled in Stratford 1638. It is still owned by his descendants. It does not seem probable this is the original house, or if so, that it has not been greatly modernized.

Avery House (N°1) Groton.

Avery House (N°2) Groton.

The Webb Mansion Wethersfield.

The Hollister House, Wethersfield

The Barnard House, Hartford.

Noah Webster's Birthplace, W. Hartford.

Gov.ᵗ Trumbulls Residence Lebanon.

Gov.ˢ Trumbulls War Office. Lebanon.

The Lynes House, Norwalk.

This is a well-preserved house on the Main Street, built by Benj. Isaacs, 1746, and now owned by the Lynes family.

Old House, Norwalk.

This is no doubt the oldest house now standing in Norwalk, and cannot be less than 150 years old, but no reliable information could be gathered respecting it.

The Old Stone Fort, Windsor.

This was built of stone and logs about 1666, and was pulled down in 1800. The above is believed to be a pretty correct representation of it.

Old School-House.

This is a sample of the school-houses in which our grandfathers received their education; and some of them made much better use of their limited privileges than many of their descendants who have studied in the palaces of the present day.

Silliman House, Bridgeport.

This stands on North Avenue, and belongs to Cyrus Silliman. It was probably built by a man named Picks-ley about 135 years ago. Said to have been a tavern originally, and that Washington once stopped here. The fence and most of the trees are omitted.

Hobart House, Fairfield.

This is a very interesting old house, now owned by Miss Annie Hobart, and erected by Justin Hobart in 1765.

Judge Swift House, Windham.

This represents the house as it was originally when occupied by Judge Swift. It has since been raised another story, and otherwise modernized. It was probably built about 1760.

The Johnson House, Putnam.

This is a very old and dilapidated building about two miles from the village of Putnam. It was probably erected by a Squire Howe about 1700, and was, during the Revolutionary war occupied by Dep. Gov. Sessions of R. I.

The Allyn House, Windsor.

This represents one of the early houses of the town of Windsor, having been built by the first Squire Allyn. It stood on Broad Street Green, nearly opposite the Moore House, but, like it, has been destroyed.

The Moore House, Windsor.

This was built before 1690 by Deacon John Moore and presented to his son on his wedding-day. It stood on Broad Street Green, and has been torn down.

The Stowe House, Milford,

This is believed to have been built about 1689. During the Revolution it was the abode of Stephen Stowe, a devoted patriot. The piazza has been omitted in the view, as that is a modern addition.

Old-Fashioned Country Store, Norwich Town.

This is a good specimen of the style of country store one hundred years ago. It was built by Jos. Carpenter in 1772, and has never been modernized.

Olmstead House, East Hartford.

This was built by Samuel Olmstead in 1770, on the site of an older house which was burnt down on a Sunday, and the frame of the present one was up by the next Saturday.

The Lynde House, Hartford.

This is on Gold Street, near Main, and was built by Dr. Jas. Lynde about 100 years ago.

The Seymour House, Hartford.

This was owned by Ex-Governor Seymour, and is probably about 150 years old.

Cluster of Old Houses, Hartford.

These form a queer group at the corner of Ann and Main Streets. The central house is said to be about 170 years old.

Griswold House, Wethersfield.

This was built by —— Denning about 200 years ago. It afterwards came into the possession of the Griswold family, and Miss Griswold now owns it.

The Butler House, Wethersfield.

This was built by Dr. Porter on the site of an old post about 1750, and was the birth-place of Chief Justice Butler. It is still owned by his descendants.

The Seelye House, Bethel, Conn.

This house was probably built about 1740 by President Seelye's (of Amherst College) great grandfather. Samuel Taylor, a graduate of Nassau Hall, and has never passed out of the possession of his descendants until recently, and was taken down 1881.

The Lord House, Old Lyme.

This was probably built in 1730 by Gen. or Col. Sheldon It is now owned by Miss Lord, her great-grandfather, J(Marvin, having bought it of a man named Sheldon. Th represents the house as it was originally.

The Washington House, Stamford, Conn.

This was a famous house during the Revolutionary War, having been the headquarters of General Lee, and Washington was frequently here. It was kept as a tavern by Capt. David Webb, and was probably 160 years old when pulled down 10 or 12 years ago.

The Hotchkiss House, Derby, Conn.

This is believed to have been built by Elijah Hotchki at least as early as 1735, if not before. It is on the mai street.

Hale's Birthplace, Coventry.

This was the birthplace of the well-known patriot Matthew Hale, who freely gave up his young life for the sake of his country.

ERRATUM.

Matthew Hale, Coventry, Conn., should be Nathan Hale.

The Trumbull House, Watertown, Conn.

This was the birthplace of Rev. John Trumbull, autho of the poem "McFingal." He was born in 1750, and th house was probably built 20 or 30 years before. It is n(now standing.

Gov. Jonathan Trumbull's Residence, Lebanon.

This was the residence of Gov. Trumbull, who was the only one of all the Royal Governors that embraced the cause of the Colonies, and to his energy and efficiency is very much of the success of the war to be accredited. Under its roof have lodged Washington, Lafayette, Dr. Franklin, Gen. Putnam, John Adams, Jefferson, etc., etc.

This house is supposed to have been built by the first Gov. Trumbull's father, about 1740. It is now owned by the heirs of Dan'l Mason.

Gov. Trumbull's War Office, Lebanon.

This building (originally a store), was used by Gov. Trumbull as his war office. It has been moved a short distance from its former location, and slightly altered. It may not be known to all that Trumbull was the original "Brother Jonathan;" this being the term frequently used by Gen. Washington when speaking of him.

The Barnard House, Hartford.

John Barnard, Grandfather of the present owner, bought this of a man named Skinner, whose ancestor is believed to have built it at least 200 years ago. It is probably the oldest house now remaining in Hartford. It stands on the west side of Retreat avenue.

Noah Webster's Birth-place, W. Hartford.

Noah Webster, the Lexicographer, was born in this house in 1758. Whether his father built it is uncertain, but he sold it with 80 acres of land in 1792 for $3500 to Noah Hurlburt, and it still remains in possession of his descendants.

Avery House (No. 1), Groton.

This is about 3½ miles from Groton Ferry on the road to Mystic, is said to have been built in 1660, by Jas. Avery, and has never passed out of the family, being now owned and occupied by Jas. D. Avery, who represents the 9th generation. It is a very interesting old house.

Avery House (No. 2), Groton.

This is another Avery House in Groton, not nearly so old as the other, having been built about 1750, by Elder Parke Avery, for his son Ebenezer. It was used as a hospital for the wounded at the battle of Groton Heights, Sept. 6, 1781.

The Webb Mansion, Wethersfield.

This house is noted for the conference which took place here May 22, 1781, between Washington, Rochambeau and other generals. At this conference were laid the plans which finally resulted in the surrender of Cornwallis at Yorktown. Jos. Webb built this house about 1750, and it is now owned by W. P. Wells.

The Hollister House, Wethersfield.

This is believed to have been built by a man named Hollister, about 200 years since. It stands about a mile from the village on the road leading to Berlin, and is owned by Putnam Hollister. It is in a very dilapidated condition.

www.ingramcontent.com/pod-product-compliance
Lightning Source LLC
Chambersburg PA
CBHW030021030726
47499CB00008B/3064